HARPER
An Imprint of HarperCollinsPublishers   www.harpercollinschildrens.com • www.petethecatbooks.com • Illustrations copyright © 2016 by James Dean

Pete the Cat's Got Class

by
James Dean

HARPER
An Imprint of HarperCollins Publishers

Pete the Cat's Got Class
Copyright © 2016 by James Dean
For information address HarperCollins Children's Books, a division of HarperCollins Publishers,
195 Broadway, New York, NY 10007.
www.harpercollinschildrens.com

Library of Congress Control Number: 2015938997
ISBN 978-0-06-230410-0

Typography by Jeanne L. Hogle
16 17 18 19 20   SCP   10 9 8 7 6 5 4 3 2 1
❖
First Edition

"It's math time," says Pete's teacher, Mr. G.
Pete the Cat loves math. He loves how
the numbers work together.

"If I add three red blocks and four yellow blocks together, how many blocks would we have in all?" says Mr. G.
Pete raises his hand.

Mr. G asks the class a subtraction question: "If I take two blocks away from seven blocks, how many blocks will be left?"

Pete raises his hand, but the teacher calls on Tom.

"Nine," says Tom.

Pete feels bad for Tom. Tom is super smart. He can name all the dinosaurs. He just has trouble with math.

Pete has an idea! He will help Tom
become awesome at math.

Helping is cool!

On the bus home from school, Pete sits next to Tom.

"Do you want to come over to play?" Tom asks. "I got some cool new race cars for my birthday."

"Awesome," says Pete. "We can do our math homework—and then we can race the cars."

"I hate math," says Tom.

"You don't hate math," Pete tells Tom.
"You just don't love it yet."

Pete sets up some blocks. "If I add five blue blocks and three orange blocks together, how many blocks will I have in all?"

"This is boring," says Tom. "Can't we play with my race cars?" This gives Pete a great idea! "Sure we can," he says.

Pete lines up some race cars. "If five red cars are going to the racetrack and five yellow cars are going to the car wash, how many cars are on the road?" he asks.

"Easy," says Tom. "Ten cars— like a traffic jam!"

"Now what if two of the cars stayed home?" Pete says.
"How many cars would be left?"
"Hmm," says Tom, studying the lineup. "Eight cars."
"Right!" says Pete. "See? I told you that math is awesome!"

Pete quizzes Tom on one math problem
after the next.

"Four cars minus one."
"Three," says Tom.

"Eight cars plus seven," says Pete.
"Fifteen," says Tom. "I can't believe it!
I'm doing math—and I'm loving it!"

Pete and Tom do their homework.

"Let me know if you need my help," says Pete.

"Thanks," says Tom, "but I know what I'm doing now."

The next day, Pete hands in his math homework. Tom does too.

After lunch, the teacher passes back their assignment. Pete and Tom each got one wrong.

"I'd like to see you two after class," Mr. G says.

"You both know not to copy someone else's homework,"
says Mr. G.

"We didn't copy," says Pete.

"You both got the exact same answer wrong,"
Mr. G tells them.

"How can we prove that we got the answers on our own?" says Tom.

"I know!" Pete tells him. "Bring your race cars to school tomorrow."
"Why?" Tom asks.
"You'll see," says Pete with a smile.

The next day, Pete and Tom get to school early.

"What are all the race cars for?" asks Mr. G.

"To show you how Tom got to be so good at math," says Pete.

"Give Tom a math problem," Pete says.
"Any math problem."

"I'll get it right," says Tom,
"without Pete's help."

Mr. G gives Tom one math problem after the other.
And Tom uses the race cars to get all the answers right.
"Wow!" says Mr. G. "I am impressed."

"Pete helped me by making math fun!" Tom says.
"I think that's something we can all learn from Pete," Mr. G says.